SHIMRI'S BIG IDEA

A Story of Ancient Jerusalem

By Elka Weber

Illustrated by Inbal Gigi Bousidan

This PJ BOOK belongs to

_____

_____

PJ Library®

JEWISH BEDTIME STORIES and SONGS

APPLES & HONEY PRESS

NOTE TO FAMILIES

Hezekiah's Tunnel is a very long tunnel, dug during the reign of King Hezekiah in the eighth century BCE, to bring water from the Gihon spring into the city of Jerusalem. It is mentioned twice in the Bible, and an inscription inside the tunnel actually marks the spot where two teams of workmen met. The tunnel is an extraordinary feat of engineering for its time, and we still do not know exactly how it was designed.

In this story, Shimri knows that big ideas can come from small mouths. Do you have a big idea for how to fix a problem or improve the world around you? What is it?

To Eli and our children, for all their big ideas –EW

To my dear, creative father, Abraham Gigi, thank you! –IGB

The publisher would like to thank Sue Melmed, Israel Museum guide,
for her help with the time period covered in the book.

Apples & Honey Press
An imprint of Behrman House
Millburn, NJ 07041
www.applesandhoneypress.com

Text copyright © 2019 by Elka Weber
Illustrations copyright © 2019 by Inbal Gigi Bousidan

ISBN 978-1-68115-541-8

Library of Congress Cataloging-in-Publication Data is available

Design by Virtual Paintbrush | Editor: Amanda Cohen

Printed in China
1 3 5 7 9 8 6 4 2

041932.6K1/B1379/A6

"No, you can't come to the fields with us. Plowing is a job for men."

Shimri watched sadly as his father and brothers left the house.

He was little, but he might have ideas for helping, he told Grandma Eliora.

"You might," she agreed. "Big ideas can come from small mouths. But there is a time for everything in this world. Right now, you need to look, listen—and learn!

And you need to clear the breakfast table."

As Shimri reached for a cup, it tipped over and the water spilled out. Before the water could fall to the ground, Grandma Eliora put her hand at the edge of the table to turn its direction.

"Look!" Shimri cried. "If you block water, it goes where you want it to go."

Grandma smiled, but Mother just shook her head. "We'll need more water. Malka, will you go down to the spring? And take Shimri, too."

"Do I have to take him? Drawing water is a job for big girls!" Malka lifted the water jug onto her strong shoulder.

"Shimri won't bother you. He's just going to look and listen. Isn't that right?" said Grandma, winking at him.

As Shimri walked with Malka, he tried not
to talk too much. They walked and walked.
It grew hotter and hotter.

At the city walls, they went through a special covered passage until at last they reached the spring.

"I wish the water came from inside the city walls!" said Shimri.

"Silly boy," replied Malka, sharply. "How can you move a spring?"

Shimri just stayed quiet.

On the way back, they passed a dark opening in a large rock. "What's that?" he wondered. "A secret tunnel?"

He ran over to it. He poked his head inside. How far did it go? But Malka was tapping her foot.

"What are you doing, crawling around in the dirt? Come on, move those little legs of yours."

When they came home, they found Mother and Grandma Eliora

holding a freshly dried sheet. They held it out at opposite ends, then walked toward each other to fold it.

"Can I help?"
asked Shimri.

"No, this is work for grown women," said his mother. "Why don't you go and play?"

So Shimri went up to the roof.
He stomped around, pretending
to be an ox plowing a field.

He bent and stood, as if he were drawing water. Then he danced back and forth as if he were folding sheets.

"Shimri!" called his mother. "What are you doing? The whole house is shaking!"

So Shimri came downstairs and took out the supper bowls. He didn't drop any of them. Grandma Eliora gave him a warm smile.

Father brought news that night. "The king wants to build a tunnel to bring the spring water inside the city walls. That way, the water will be closer to us all."

"I'd like that," said Malka, rubbing her shoulder.

"Tomorrow he is gathering his wisest men. They need to come up with a plan," Father said.

Shimri thought about his day. He thought about how he had watched and listened, and learned.

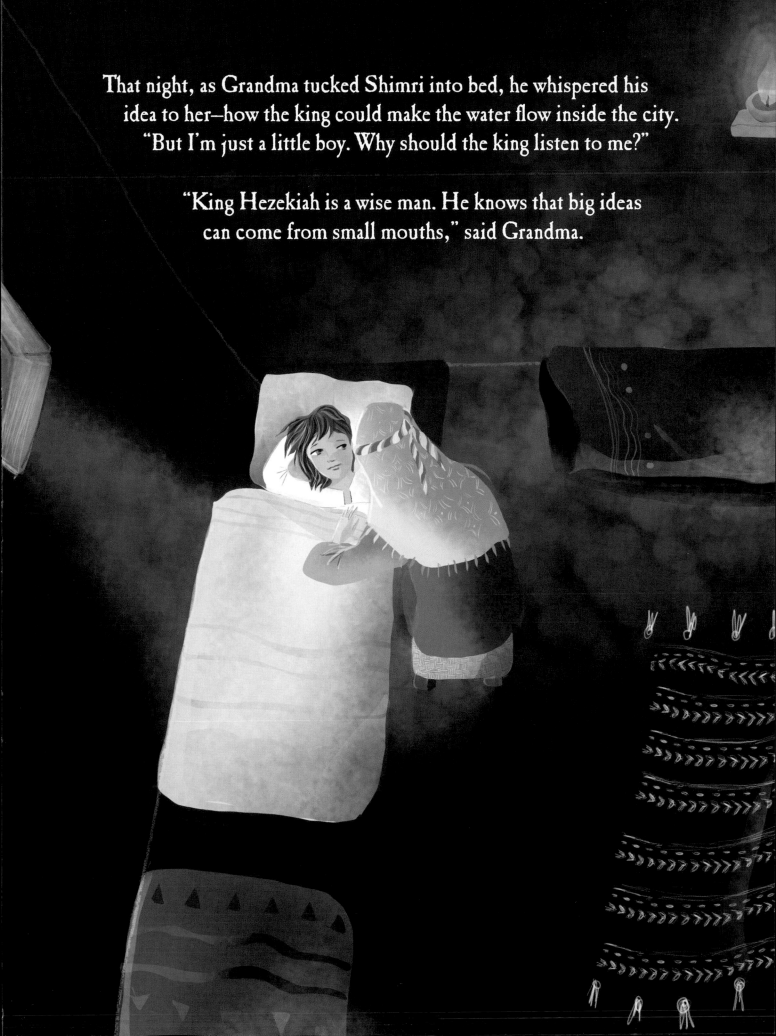

That night, as Grandma tucked Shimri into bed, he whispered his
idea to her—how the king could make the water flow inside the city.
"But I'm just a little boy. Why should the king listen to me?"

"King Hezekiah is a wise man. He knows that big ideas
can come from small mouths," said Grandma.

So, early next morning—while Mother and Grandma were cooking, Malka was on her way to the spring, and Father and the boys were busy in the fields—Shimri set off for the highest part of the city and the king's palace.

At the gates
stood a tall,
strong guard.

Shimri cleared his throat. "I'm here to advise the king about how to build a tunnel."

"You?" said the guard, looking him up and down. "You seem a little . . . young to be a tunnel expert."

"I am," said Shimri. "But I have an idea. And big ideas can come from small mouths."

King Hezekiah and Queen Hepzibah
were taking a morning stroll in the
palace gardens.

They stopped when
they saw Shimri. The
queen whispered
something to the king,
who nodded.
"Let him in,"
said the king.

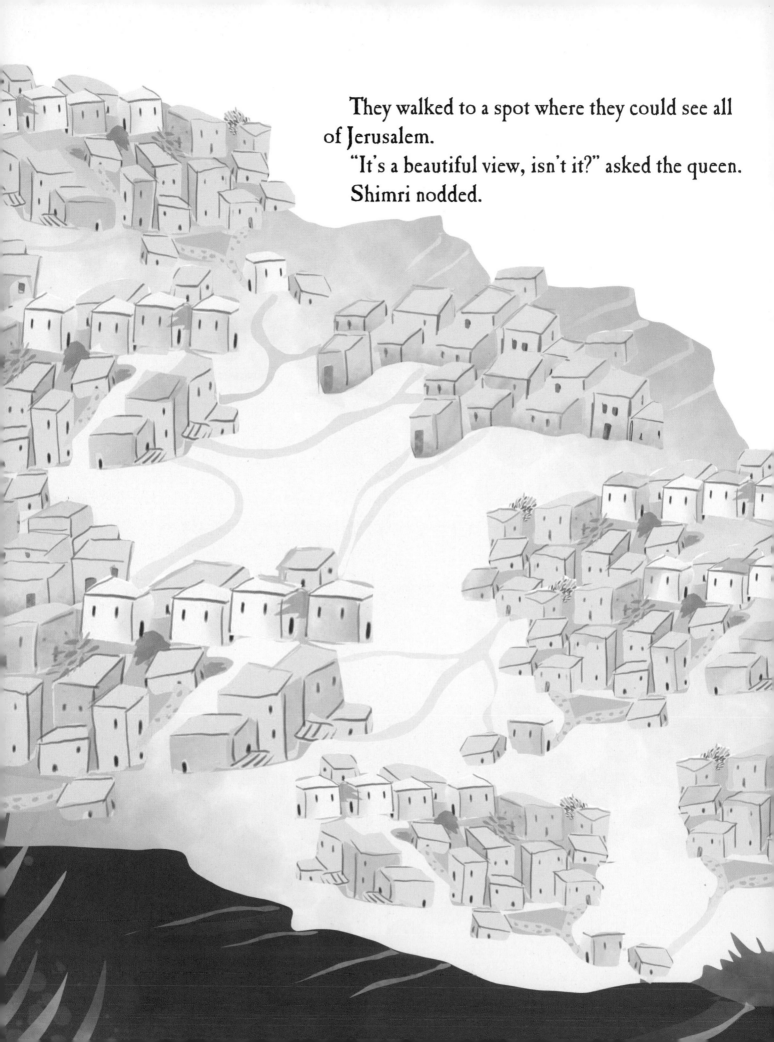

They walked to a spot where they could see all of Jerusalem.

"It's a beautiful view, isn't it?" asked the queen.

Shimri nodded.

King Hezekiah smiled. "Now, tell us who you are. And how you got to be an expert on tunnel building."

Shimri took a deep breath.

"My name is Shimri, son of Azaria. I have been watching my family doing their work—watching them, and learning."

"Everyone knows that you can make water go where you want by blocking its path, right?"

"That is true," said the queen. Shimri wondered if she had ever kept water from spilling off a table.

He went on. "Yesterday, when I went down to the spring with my sister to draw water, I noticed a large crack in the rock."

"Yes . . . I used to play there when I was a boy," said the king. His smile had a faraway look.

"Well," Shimri went on, "surely it wouldn't be difficult to dig out a tunnel there?"

"You could break the crack open wider and carve a tunnel out of the rock, under the city walls. Then water could flow through the tunnel—for everyone."

King Hezekiah rubbed his chin. "It sounds like a good idea, but won't it take a very long time to dig a tunnel that long?"

Shimri nodded wisely, remembering his mother and grandmother folding a sheet together. "You'll need two teams of workers. One will dig from the north and the other from the south, and they can meet in the middle."

"But they'll be working underground in the dark," said the king. "How will the two groups meet each other?"

"Oh, for that you will need a lot of noise."

"A lot of noise?" asked the queen.

"Yes. When a child jumps around on the roof of a house, people inside the house hear the noise. You'll need workers above ground to make noise. The tunnel diggers will hear the noise above them, and they'll follow the sound. That's how they will meet in the middle."

The king leaned back in his chair. "You know, I'm beginning to think this idea could work."

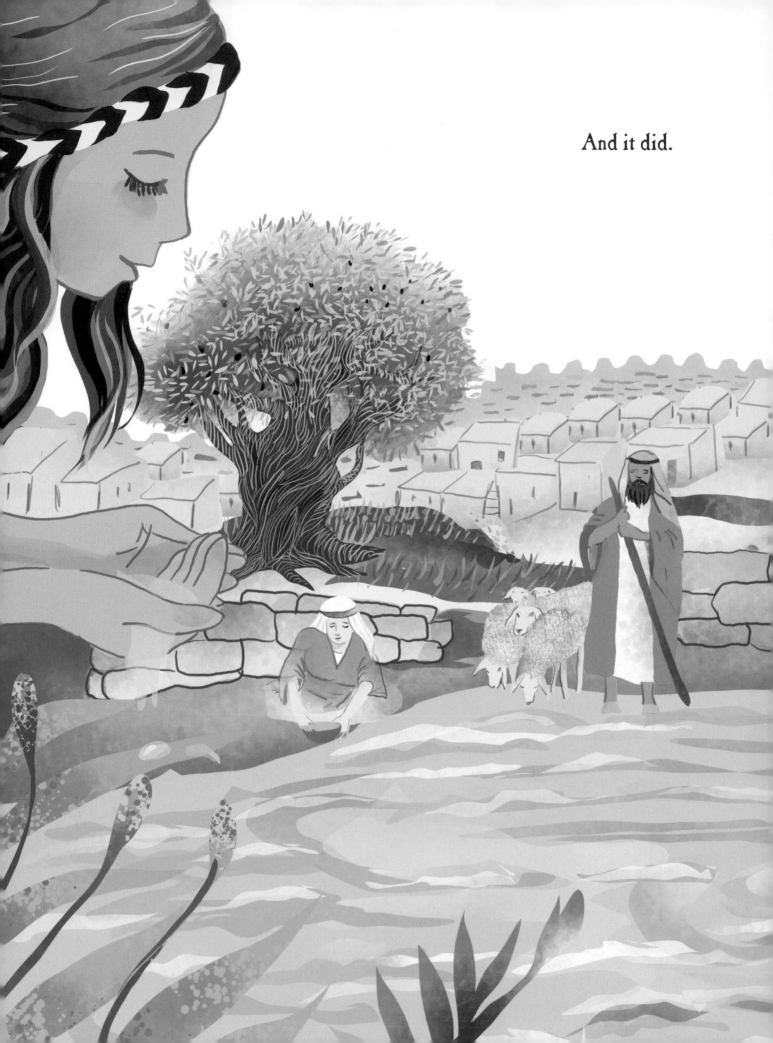

And it did.

The tunnel was dug, water flowed through it, and the people of Jerusalem could draw water without leaving the city. Everyone learned that big ideas can come from small mouths.

"But we knew that already, didn't we?" said Grandma Eliora.